LITTLE GOLDEN BOOK® CLASSICS
Featuring the art of
Gustaf Tenggren

Three Best-Loved Tales

THUMBELINA
By Hans Christian Andersen

TAWNY SCRAWNY LION
By Kathryn Jackson

THE POKY LITTLE PUPPY
By Janette Sebring Lowrey

A GOLDEN BOOK • NEW YORK
Western Publishing Company, Inc., Racine, Wisconsin 53404

THUMBELINA

By Hans Christian Andersen

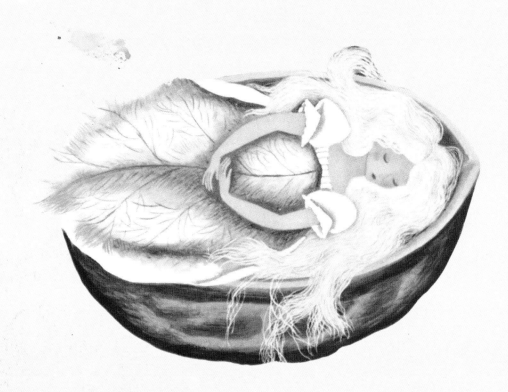

There was once a tiny little girl. She was sweet and pretty and no taller than your thumb, so Thumbelina was her given name.

A nicely varnished walnut shell made a bed for her, with a violet petal mattress and a rose leaf coverlet.

That was where she slept at night; but in the daytime she played about in a small dish garden, where she rowed her tulip-petal boat from side to side of a tiny flower-wreathed lake.

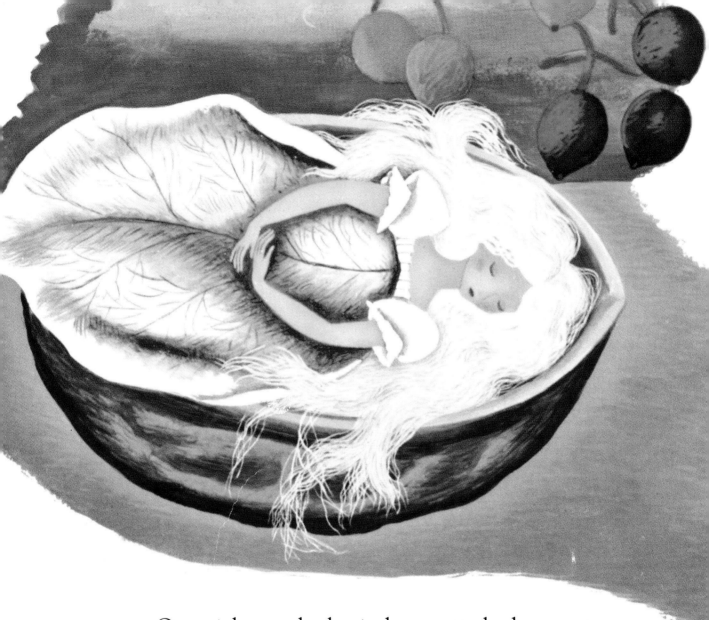

One night, as she lay in her pretty bed, a great ugly toad came hopping in through the open window and jumped straight to the table where Thumbelina was lying asleep.

"She would make just the wife for my son," thought the toad. So she snatched up Thumbelina, walnut shell and all, and hopped off with her back to the garden.

There, in the muddy bank of a wide brook, the toad made her home with her ugly son. Now, while she decorated a room in their house with rushes and leaves for her daughter-in-law, the mother toad left Thumbelina, in her walnut-shell bed, on a water-lily leaf floating on the brook.

In the morning, when the poor little thing woke up, and saw where she was, she cried most bitterly. For the big green leaf had water all around it, so she could not possibly escape.

The little fishes, swimming in the water below, heard her crying. They had caught sight of the ugly mother toad, and they knew what she had in mind. So they all swarmed around the tough green stalk that held Thumbelina's leaf, and they gnawed it through with their teeth. Then the leaf carried Thumbelina far down the brook.

At last her leaf boat stopped against a mossy bank in a strange forest world.

She had no way to travel farther, so all through the summer Thumbelina lived quite alone in that enormous wood. From blades of grass she wove a bed. This she hung neatly under a leaf, where she was sheltered from the rain.

For food she had honey from the flowers, for drink, the morning dew on the leaves. And so she passed the summer and autumn.

Then came winter—the bitter winter. All the
birds flew away; the flowers withered. The great leaf
under which she had lain shriveled to a faded yellow
stalk.

As Thumbelina searched for a new shelter, it
began to snow, and every snowflake that fell on her
was as if a whole shovelful were thrown on one of
us, so delicate and tiny was she.

On the fringe of the wood, she came at last to a field mouse's door. Down below the stubble of a large cornfield, the field mouse had a fine snug house with a whole storeroom full of corn.

"You poor little thing!" said the kindly field mouse when she found Thumbelina shivering at her door. "Come into my warm room and have a bite with me."

The mouse took a liking to Thumbelina at once and invited her to stay for the winter.

"Just so you keep my rooms tidy and nice and tell me stories," she said.

Thumbelina agreed and was comfortable there.

In the evenings the field mouse's neighbor often
came to call. He was a tiresome old mole.

"But his house is even snugger than mine," the
mouse said, "and he wears such a lovely black velvet
coat. If only you could get him for a husband, you'd
be well off indeed."

Thumbelina paid no attention to this. She had no intention of marrying the mole. He was very learned, she agreed, but he couldn't bear sunshine and flowers and said all sorts of rude things about them, though he had never seen them.

Now he had dug a long passage from his house to theirs. And there Thumbelina found a bird one day—a swallow, numb with cold and almost dead.

She wove a fine big blanket of hay and she spread it over the swallow and tucked some cotton wool in at the sides. She brought him water in the petal of a flower and took care of him all winter long.

When she was not caring for the swallow,
Thumbelina spent her time spinning and weaving
on her trousseau with the help of some spiders. For
the tiresome mole had proposed to her, and the
mouse decided they should be married soon.

Poor Thumbelina! She grew sadder and sadder as the wedding day drew near. She would have to say good-bye to the sun and the flowers, since the mole did not care for them.

When spring arrived, bringing her wedding day, and the sun began to warm the earth, Thumbelina opened a hole in the roof of the passage, and the swallow stepped out into the pleasant sunshine.

She watched him with tears in her eyes.

"Come with me, Thumbelina," he begged, for he could not bear to have her marry the mole and live forever underground. "You can sit on my back and we shall fly far away to the warm countries, where it is always summer, with lovely flowers."

"Yes," said Thumbelina of a sudden, "I will come with you." She climbed on the bird's back, settled her feet on his wings, and tied her sash firmly to his feathers. Then the swallow flew high up into the air, over lakes and forests, high up over the mountains of everlasting snow.

At last they reached the warm countries, where

grapes grew on sunny walls and slopes and
lemons and oranges ripened in the groves.

The swallow flew on, while the country became
more and more beautiful, until at last they came to
an ancient palace of shining marble standing
among green trees beside a blue lake. Here the
swallow flew down with Thumbelina.

He placed her on a broad flower petal—

and there, in the middle of the flower, was a little
man no bigger than herself. He was the King of
the spirits of the flowers.

"My, how handsome he is!" Thumbelina thought. And the little King was equally enchanted at the sight of her. He took the crown from his own head and placed it on hers. Then he asked her what her name might be and if she would be his wife.

She knew at once he was the husband for her, so
she said Yes to the King. Then from every flower
round about a tiny lady or gentleman appeared.
Each of them brought a gift for the new queen, but
her favorite of all was a pair of beautiful wings from
a white butterfly. These they fastened to her back
so that she could flit with the others from flower to
flower.

Such rejoicing as there was then! And the swallow sat in his nest above and sang for their happiness with all his loving heart.

TAWNY
SCRAWNY
LION

By Kathryn Jackson

Once there was a tawny, scrawny, hungry lion
who never could get enough to eat.

He chased monkeys on Monday—

kangaroos on Tuesday—

zebras on Wednesday—

bears on Thursday—

camels on Friday—

and on Saturday, elephants!

And since he caught everything he ran after, that lion should have been as fat as butter. But he wasn't at all. The more he ate, the scrawnier and hungrier he grew.

The other animals didn't feel one bit safe. They stood at a distance and tried to talk things over with the tawny, scrawny lion.

"It's all your fault for running away," he grumbled.
"If I didn't have to run, run, run for every single bite
I get, I'd be fat as butter and sleek as satin.

Then I wouldn't have to eat so much, and you'd last longer!"

Just then, a fat little rabbit came hopping through the forest, picking berries. All the big animals looked at him and grinned slyly.

"Rabbit," they said. "Oh, you lucky rabbit! We appoint you to talk things over with the lion."

That made the little rabbit feel very proud.
"What shall I talk about?" he asked eagerly.
"Any old thing," said the big animals. "The important thing is to go right up close."
So the fat little rabbit hopped right up to the big hungry lion and counted his ribs.

"You look much too scrawny to talk things over,"
he said. "So how about supper at my house first?"

"What's for supper?" asked the lion.
The little rabbit said, "Carrot stew." That
sounded awful to the lion. But the little rabbit said,
"Yes, sir, my five fat sisters and my four fat

brothers are making a delicious big carrot stew right now!"

"What are we waiting for?" cried the lion. And he went hopping away with the little rabbit, thinking of ten fat rabbits and looking just as jolly as you please.

"Well," grinned all the big animals. "That should take care of Tawny Scrawny for today."

Before very long, the lion began to wonder if they would ever get to the rabbit's house.

First, the fat little rabbit kept stopping to pick berries and mushrooms and all sorts of good-smelling herbs. And when his basket was full, what did he do but flop down on the riverbank!

"Wait a bit," he said. "I want to catch a few

fish for the stew."

That was almost too much for the hungry lion.

For a moment, he thought he would have to eat that one little rabbit then and there. But he kept saying, "Five fat sisters and four fat brothers" over and over to himself. And at last the two were on their way again.

"Here we are!" said the rabbit, hopping around a turn with the lion close behind him. Sure enough, there was the rabbit's house, with a big pot of carrot stew bubbling over an open fire.

And sure enough, there were nine more fat, merry little rabbits hopping around it!

When they saw the fish, they popped them into the stew, along with the mushrooms and herbs. The stew began to smell very good indeed.

And when they saw the tawny, scrawny lion, they gave him a big bowl of hot stew. And then they hopped about so busily that, really, it would have been quite a job for that tired, hungry lion to catch even one of them!

So he gobbled his stew, but the rabbits filled his bowl again. When he had eaten all he could hold, they heaped his bowl with berries.

And when the berries were gone—the tawny, scrawny lion wasn't scrawny anymore! He felt so good and fat and comfortable that he couldn't even move.

"Here's a fine thing!" he said to himself. "All these fat little rabbits, and I haven't room inside for even one!"

He looked at all those fine, fat little rabbits and wished he'd get hungry again.

"Mind if I stay awhile?" he asked.

"We wouldn't even hear of your going!" said the rabbits. Then they plumped themselves down in the lion's lap and began to sing songs.

And somehow, even when it was time to say
good night, that lion wasn't one bit hungry!

Home he went, through the soft moonlight,
singing softly to himself. He curled up in his bed,
patted his sleek, fat tummy, and smiled.

When he woke up in the morning, it was
Monday.

"Time to chase monkeys!" said the lion.

But he wasn't one bit hungry for monkeys! What he wanted was some more of that tasty carrot stew. So off he went to visit the rabbits.

On Tuesday he didn't want kangaroos, and on Wednesday he didn't want zebras. He wasn't hungry for bears on Thursday, or camels on Friday, or elephants on Saturday.

All the big animals were so surprised and happy!

They dressed in their best and went to see the fat little rabbit.

"Rabbit," they said. "Oh, you wonderful rabbit! What in the world did you talk to the tawny, scrawny, hungry, terrible lion about?"

The fat little rabbit jumped up in the air and said, "Oh, my goodness! We had such a good time with that nice, jolly lion that I guess we forgot to talk about anything at all!"

And before the big animals could say one word, the tawny lion came skipping up the path. He had a basket of berries for the fat rabbit sisters, and a string of fish for the fat rabbit brothers, and a big bunch of daisies for the fat rabbit himself.

"I came for supper," he said, shaking paws all around.

Then he sat down in the soft grass, looking fat as butter, sleek as satin, and jolly as all get-out, all ready for another good big supper of carrot stew.

THE
POKY
LITTLE
PUPPY

By Janette Sebring Lowrey

Five little puppies dug a hole under the fence and went for a walk in the wide, wide world.

Through the meadow they went, down the road, over the bridge, across the green grass, and up the hill, one after the other.

And when they got to the top of the hill, they counted themselves: one, two, three, four. One little puppy wasn't there.

"Now where in the world is that poky little puppy?" they wondered. For he certainly wasn't on top of the hill.

He wasn't going down the other side. The only thing they could see going down was a fuzzy caterpillar.

He wasn't coming up this side. The only thing
they could see coming up was a quick green lizard.

But when they looked down at the grassy place
near the bottom of the hill, there he was, running
round and round, his nose to the ground.

"What is he doing?" the four little puppies asked
one another. And down they went to see, roly-poly,
pell-mell, tumble-bumble, till they came to the
green grass; and there they stopped short.

"What in the world are you doing?" they asked.

"I smell something!" said the poky little puppy.

Then the four little puppies began to sniff, and they smelled it, too.

"Rice pudding!" they said.

And home they went, as fast as they could go, over the bridge, up the road, through the meadow, and under the fence. And there, sure enough, was dinner waiting for them, with rice pudding for dessert.

But their mother was greatly displeased. "So you're the little puppies who dig holes under fences!" she said. "No rice pudding tonight!" And she made them go straight to bed.

But the poky little puppy came home after everyone was sound asleep.

He ate up the rice pudding and crawled into bed as happy as a lark.

The next morning someone had filled the hole and put up a sign. The sign said:

DON'T EVER DIG HOLES UNDER THIS FENCE!

BUT…

The five little puppies dug a hole under the fence, just the same, and went for a walk in the wide, wide world.

Through the meadow they went, down the road, over the bridge, across the green grass, and up the hill, two and two. And when they got to the top of the hill, they counted themselves: one, two, three, four. One little puppy wasn't there.

"Now where in the world is that poky little puppy?" they wondered. For he certainly wasn't on top of the hill.

He wasn't going down the other side. The only thing they could see going down was a big black spider.

He wasn't coming up this side. The only thing
they could see coming up was a brown hoptoad.

But when they looked down at the grassy place
near the bottom of the hill, there was the poky
little puppy, sitting still as a stone, with his head
on one side and his ears cocked up.

"What is he doing?" the four little puppies asked
one another. And down they went to see, roly-poly,
pell-mell, tumble-bumble, till they came to the
green grass; and there they stopped short.

"What in the world are you doing?" they asked.

"I hear something!" said the poky little puppy.

The four little puppies listened, and they could
hear it, too. "Chocolate custard!" they cried.
"Someone is spooning it into our bowls!"

And home they went, as fast as they could go, over the bridge, up the road, through the meadow, and under the fence. And there, sure enough, was dinner waiting for them, with chocolate custard for dessert.

But their mother was greatly displeased. "So you're the little puppies who will dig holes under fences!" she said. "No chocolate custard tonight!" And she made them go straight to bed.

But the poky little puppy came home after everyone else was sound asleep, and he ate up all

the chocolate custard and crawled into bed as happy as a lark.

The next morning someone had filled the hole and put up a sign.

The sign said:

BUT…

In spite of that, the five little puppies dug a hole under the fence and went for a walk in the wide, wide world.

Through the meadow they went, down the road, over the bridge, across the green grass, and up the hill, two and two. And when they got to the top of the hill, they counted themselves: one, two, three, four. One little puppy wasn't there.

"Now where in the world is that poky little puppy?" they wondered. For he certainly wasn't on top of the hill.

He wasn't going down the other side. The only thing they could see going down was a little grass snake.

He wasn't coming up this side. The only thing
they could see coming up was a big grasshopper.

But when they looked down at the grassy place
near the bottom of the hill, there he was, looking
hard at something on the ground in front of him.

"What is he doing?" the four little puppies asked
one another. And down they went to see, roly-poly,
pell-mell, tumble-bumble, till they came to the
green grass; and there they stopped short.

"What in the world are you doing?" they asked.

"I see something!" said the poky little puppy.

The four little puppies looked, and they could see it, too. It was a ripe red strawberry growing there in the grass.

"Strawberry shortcake!" they cried.

And home they went, as fast as they could go, over the bridge, up the road, through the meadow, and under the fence. And there, sure enough, was dinner waiting for them, with strawberry shortcake for dessert.

But their mother said: "So you're the little puppies who dug that hole under the fence again! No strawberry shortcake for supper tonight!" And she made them go straight to bed.

But the four little puppies waited till they thought she was asleep, and then they slipped out and filled up the hole, and when they turned around, there was their mother watching them.

"What good little puppies!" she said. "Come have some strawberry shortcake!"

And this time, when the poky little puppy got home, he had to squeeze in through a wide place in the fence. And there were his four brothers and sisters, licking the last crumbs from their saucer.

"Dear me!" said his mother. "What a pity you're so poky! Now the strawberry shortcake is all gone!"

So poky little puppy had to go to bed without a single bite of shortcake, and he felt very sorry for himself.

And the next morning someone had put up a sign that read:

NO DESSERTS EVER UNLESS PUPPIES NEVER DIG HOLES UNDER THIS FENCE AGAIN!

About Gustaf Tenggren

This highly talented illustrator was born in Magra, Sweden, in 1896. Both his father and grandfather were artists. Gustaf Tenggren once described the influence his grandfather especially had had on him. "Summers were happily spent in the country," he said, "tagging along with my grandfather, who was a woodcarver and painter and also a fine companion for a small boy. I never tired of watching him carve or mix the colors he used."

The young Tenggren entered art school at the age of thirteen. Before he was twenty or had yet graduated from the art school in Gothenburg, he was commissioned to illustrate his first children's book. Three years later he emigrated to the United States, settling finally in New York. "For many years," he said, "my studio was in this great city." As the years passed, he grew increasingly popular as a children's book illustrator.

In the late 1930s Gustaf Tenggren worked at the Disney Studio in California, designing both characters and backgrounds for such classic Disney films as *Snow White* and *Pinocchio*. After working with Disney, Tenggren devoted himself exclusively to children's books, including more than two dozen rich and varied titles for Golden Books.

The Poky Little Puppy, included in this volume, was one of the first twelve Little Golden Books ever published. It was Tenggren's most successful book as well. Over thirteen million copies of *Poky* have been printed since 1942. Aside from his fanciful animal books, Gustaf Tenggren also illustrated major classical works for Golden, including *Tales From the Arabian Nights, The Canterbury Tales of Geoffrey Chaucer,* and *King Arthur and the Knights of the Round Table.*

The gifted artist, who died in 1970, was once asked what children's book illustration meant to him. "I find this work very rewarding," he answered, "as it seems to give so much pleasure to so many children."